TRACKER
On the Job

by Liam O'Donnell   Illustrated by Robert Hynes

For Sara and Ducky, two friends that will never be separated — L.O.

To Marc Moyens — R.H.

Book Copyright © 2004 Trudy Corporation

Published by Soundprints Division of Trudy Corporation, Norwalk, Connecticut.

Book design: Marcin D. Pilchowski
Editor: Laura Gates Galvin
Editorial assistance: Brian E. Giblin

First Edition 2004
10 9 8 7 6 5 4 3 2 1
Printed in China

Acknowledgements:
    Soundprints would like to thank Joanne Clevenger and all the helpful staff and veterinarians at the American Veterinary Medical Association.

Library of Congress Cataloging-in-Publication Data

O'Donnell, Liam, 1970-
    Tracker : on the job / by Liam O'Donnell ; illustrated by Robert Hynes.--1st ed.
        p. cm. -- (Pet tales)
    Summary: On her first day on the job, Tracker, a German shepherd search and rescue dog, makes a young girl happy by finding her lost toy.
    ISBN 1-59249-293-2 (large pbk.) -- ISBN 1-59249-294-0 (small pbk.)
        [1. Police dogs--Fiction. 2. German shepherd dog--Fiction. 3. Dogs--Fiction.
    4. Lost and found possessions--Fiction.] I. Hynes, Robert, ill. II. Title. III. Series.

PZ7.O2397Tr 2004
[E]--dc22

                                                                                    2004002648

TRACKER
On the Job

by Liam O'Donnell   Illustrated by Robert Hynes

Soundprints

It's a sunny summer morning and all is quiet in Tracker's house. But the young German Shepherd is wide-awake. With her nose, she gently nudges her sleeping owner. Tracker is a search-and-rescue dog and today is her first day at her new job.

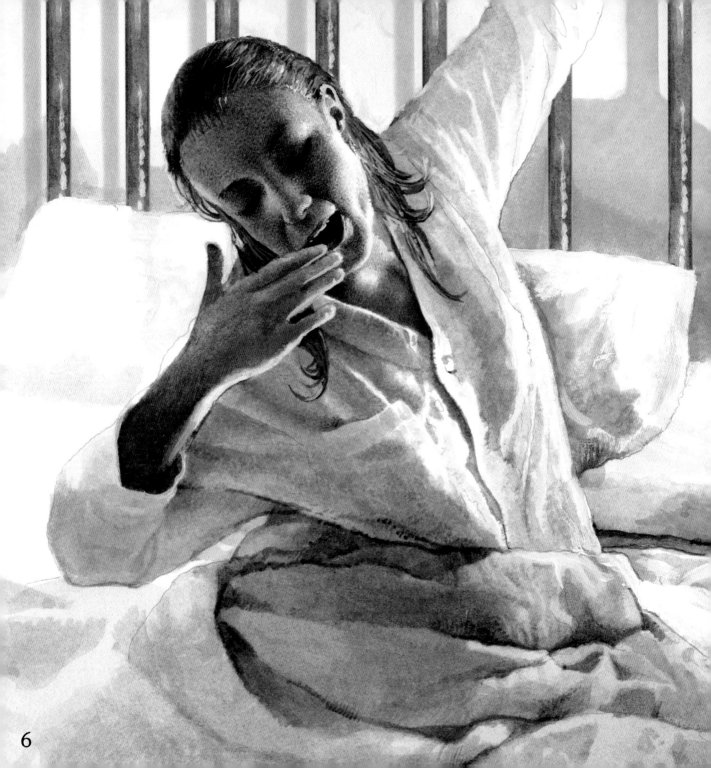

Tracker's partner, Officer Megan, sits up and stretches. Tracker and Officer Megan went to a special school together to become a search-and-rescue team. After many weeks of training, and a careful checkup by her veterinarian, Tracker is ready to start her first day of work—but Megan is still in her pajamas!

Tracker follows Officer Megan into the kitchen. Officer Megan scoops a healthy helping of dog food into a big bowl. Tracker smells her yummy breakfast! Her keen sense of smell helps her as a search-and-rescue dog. She uses her nose to follow scents and help police officers find missing things, including missing people.

After Officer Megan gets dressed, Tracker climbs into a special police car. She has plenty of room in the back. There are no toys in the car because Tracker is on duty and she must be ready for action at all times. Today, Tracker is going to meet her co-workers for the first time.

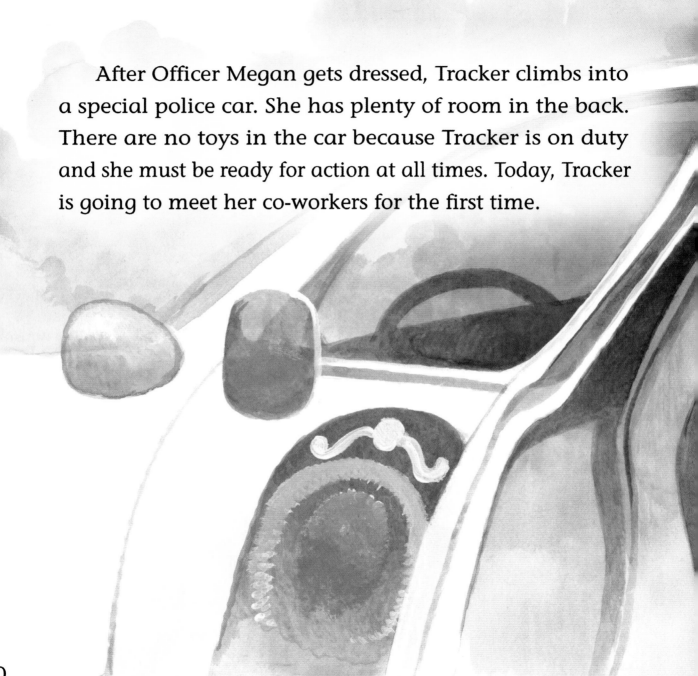

Inside the police station, Tracker is greeted by the officers. She sniffs each of them and remembers their scents. The police sergeant assigns the day's duties. There is a farmer's market in the park today. Tracker and Officer Megan will spend the morning patrolling the town. Then they will go to the park and visit the market.

Officer Megan drives along a flat country road, passing farms and golden wheat fields. Tracker loves feeling the wind in her face. She is tempted to stick her nose out the window, but she stops herself. It is unsafe for dogs to stick their heads out of car windows. There will be plenty of time for play when the workday is done.

15

Tracker and Officer Megan arrive at the farmer's market. The park is crowded and the air is filled with the sweet smell of baked pies. Tracker wants to run into the park and join the fun, but she stays with Officer Megan. She is well trained and always waits for her partner's command before moving.

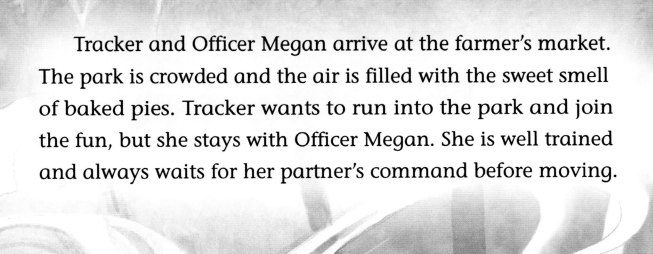

Tracker and Officer Megan walk slowly through the crowd. Proud farmers display fresh fruit, colorful vegetables and homemade jams. People wander through the park, munching corn on the cob, eating ice cream and enjoying the summer day. But one little girl, Sara, is too sad to enjoy the fun. She has lost her favorite stuffed toy, Ducky.

When Sara sees Tracker and Officer Megan, she wipes away her tears. Sara lost Ducky somewhere in the park. Officer Megan offers to help. Tracker can practice her new training and find Ducky. Since Sara and Ducky are almost always together, they will smell the same to Tracker. Tracker sniffs Sara's jacket and picks up the missing toy's scent.

With Ducky's scent in her nose, Tracker is ready to search. She sniffs through the grass, quickly moving from tree to tree. Officer Megan will know when Tracker has located the scent just by watching her. The park is full of different smells and Tracker is having trouble finding Ducky's scent.

But Tracker doesn't give up. She sniffs her way past the delicious smells of Mr. Galloway's hot dog stand and follows her nose into the playground. She is moving more slowly now. This tells Officer Megan that Tracker has found Ducky's scent. Tracker sniffs around the sandpit, under the swings, and stops at the foot of the slide. She raises her head and quietly sits down.

Tracker has found Ducky! Sara races to pick up Ducky from the ground. Her favorite toy is back and her tears are gone. Sara asks Officer Megan if she can give Tracker a big hug. Tracker also gets an approving rub and a treat from Officer Megan.

For the rest of the day, Tracker walks through the park bursting with pride. When they get home, Tracker is tired from all her hard work. She is ready for bed now, but tomorrow she will once again help her new community!

Pet Health and Safety Tips

- Some dogs help people stay healthy by serving as guides for the visually- and hearing-impaired; participating in search-and-rescue work during a disaster; or working as therapy dogs in hospitals, long-term care facilities, and assisted-living programs. These animals undergo special training to ensure that they are well qualified to perform their important tasks.

- Veterinarians, technicians, and others who work in animal hospitals may also volunteer to serve on Veterinary Medical Assistance Teams (VMATs). These teams are ready at a moment's notice to provide veterinary care to injured animals and protect public health during disasters. See www.avma.org/disaster/vmat to learn more about VMAT teams.

- Adding a new pet to your household is a big decision. Do you want a pet who will be a playful companion, or do you prefer a couch potato? Do you live in a house, apartment or condominium? Your veterinarian can help you determine which pet might best fit your family's lifestyle.

GLOSSARY

Scent: A specific kind of odor.

Team: A group of people and/or animals who work together.

Patrol: To move around an area observing or protecting it.

A Real-Life Pet Tale

Officer Robin Shelton and Brody are a dog-detective team for the Police K9 Unit in Richmond, Virginia. Brody is a seven-year-old Golden Retriever who uses his nose to help keep his town safe. Brody loves meeting the children at schools and hospitals where he and Officer Robin visit and talk about the important work they do for the Police K9 team. Brody has to stay fit and healthy to do his job and his favorite treats are crunchy doggy biscuits. When he's not working, Brody enjoys splashing around in a wading pool in his backyard.